Graveyard Diaries

ALL IN A NIGHT'S WORK

magic wagon

by Baron Specter
illustrated by Setch Kneupper

visit us at www.abdopublishing.com

Published by Magic Wagon, a division of the ABDO Group, PO Box 398166, Minneapolis, MN 55439. Copyright © 2013 by Abdo Consulting Group, Inc. International copyrights reserved in all countries. All rights reserved. No part of this book may be reproduced in any form without written permission from the publisher.

Calico Chapter Books™ is a trademark and logo of Magic Wagon.

Printed in the United States of America, North Mankato, Minnesota.
052012
092012
 This book contains at least 10% recycled materials.

Text by Baron Specter
Illustrations by Setch Kneupper
Edited by Stephanie Hedlund and Rochelle Baltzer
Interior layout and design by Neil Klinepier
Cover design by Neil Klinepier

Library of Congress Cataloging-in-Publication Data

Specter, Baron, 1957-
  All in a night's work / by Baron Specter ; illustrated by Setch Kneupper.
    p. cm. -- (Graveyard diaries ; bk. 6)
  Summary: When he accidentally trips over a grave Stan Summer lands in the middle of a century-old feud between two rival ghost families, and finds himself cast in the role of peacemaker.
  ISBN 978-1-61641-903-5
  1. Ghost stories. 2. Haunted cemeteries--Juvenile fiction. 3. Vendetta--Juvenile fiction. [1. Ghosts--Fiction. 2. Haunted places--Fiction. 3. Vendetta--Fiction. 4. Mystery and detective stories.] I. Kneupper, Setch, ill. II. Title.
  PZ7.S741314All 2012
  813.6--dc23
                                              2011052033

CONTENTS

WoodLand Cemetery
Jared's House
Marshfield Grove
Barry's House
MARSHFIELD

Chapter 1:
Happy Death Day

Stan was very late for dinner. He began to run. The shortest way home was through Hilltop Cemetery.

I promised I would be on time, Stan thought. He ran up one hill and down another. He would be at least 30 minutes late.

Stan could see his house in the distance. He crossed a grave site, tripped, and fell down hard.

Stan pushed himself up. In front of his face was an old gravestone. It said

RANDALL FORTIN.

Stan stood and brushed some dirt from his jeans. Then he looked closer at the gravestone. Randall Fortin had died on September 24.

That's today, Stan thought. *One hundred years ago. Exactly.*

"Happy birthday," Stan said with a laugh. "I mean, happy death day." Then he started walking down the hill toward home.

"How dare you laugh at me!" cried a scratchy voice.

Stan stopped walking. The voice sounded old and mean. It gave him a chill.

There was no one in sight. But the voice had been close by.

"Who's there?" Stan asked.

The voice spoke again. "Stay off of my grave, Wyman!"

"I'm not Wyman," Stan said. "I'm Stan Summer." He turned around, still looking for the person who was speaking. But Stan didn't see anyone.

Stan pointed to a group of gravestones about fifty yards away. "The Wyman graves are over there," he said.

"And that's where you Wymans should stay!" the voice said. "Stop bothering us. You don't belong over here."

"I'm not bothering anyone," Stan said. He waved his hand toward his house. "I live right over there."

"You stomped on my grave!" the voice said.

"I fell," Stan said. He took a step back. Was he speaking to Randall Fortin?

"I didn't mean to stomp on your grave. I tripped over something. I was late."

"We're all late," the voice said. "You have no reason to be over here. Go back to the Wymans. And stay there."

Stan was scared, but he laughed. Why would he stay by the Wymans? He decided to walk over to the Wyman graves and take a look. He was already late for dinner. A few more minutes wouldn't matter.

Stan circled around an overgrown area of bushes and weeds. There were no gravestones there.

The Wyman family plot was about the size of one of Stan's sixth grade classrooms at school. It had a low, rusted iron fence. Stan stepped through the open gate. Tall, thick trees surrounded the site.

There were about two dozen Wyman gravestones. Most were big blocks of granite. A few were much smaller. Stan could tell from the birth and death dates that the smaller ones were for children.

The gravestones were cracked. Lichen and moss covered some of them.

In the center of the plot stood a taller monument. It listed several Wyman family members. All had been dead for more than a hundred years.

Stan could see the Fortin graves across the brushy field. There were about twenty of them close together.

Stan leaned against the iron fence. He reached into his pocket and took out a small notepad. He needed to write some things down to share with the Zombie Hunters.

The Zombie Hunters were a group of kids who each lived on the edge of a different graveyard. They had battled ghosts and other spirits many times.

Stan's Journal: Thursday, September 24. 6:32 p.m.

I've been warned by a ghost! Randall Fortin has been dead for a hundred years. But he's up and kicking tonight. He told me to stay away from his grave. He thinks I'm one of the Wymans. Sounds as if the Fortins and the Wymans don't like each other very much. I wonder why. It might be fun to find out. I'll get the Zombie Hunters out here and we'll see what happens.

Stan read a few of the names on the gravestones:

PATRICK WYMAN
At rest

LUCILLE WYMAN BAKER
At peace

JACOB WYMAN
Called to Heaven

He heard another shout. "Stan!"
That was no ghost. It was his father.
"I'm on my way!" Stan yelled back. He cut through the brushy area to save time. The sky was nearly dark, so it was hard to see. He stumbled over some roots, but he didn't fall.

When he reached the Fortin area, he looked up. A ghost was floating near Randall's grave. It was staring at Stan. It

was pale gray and Stan could see through
it.

"You'll pay for trespassing," the ghost
said. It sounded like the one who had
spoken before. It pointed to the brushy
area Stan had crossed. "That area is ours.
No Wymans are ever welcome there.
Never return, or you will suffer."

Stan heard another ghostly voice. This
one was coming from near the Wyman

graves. "You'll do more than suffer," it said. "You'll die!"

Stan gulped. He turned and ran as hard as he could.

He'd been caught in the middle of a hundred-year-old feud.

Chapter 2:
A Ghost Orchard

Stan's Journal: Thursday, September 24. 10:05 p.m.

I wonder what's so special about that brushy area. The Fortins think it's their land. It sounds like the Wymans don't agree. Are the Wymans still haunting the cemetery, too?

There were four cemeteries in the town of Marshfield, which was sometimes called "Graveyard City." Stan lived by Hilltop Cemetery, and Amy was his neighbor. Jared lived on the edge of Woodland Cemetery. Mitch's house was next to Evergreen Cemetery. Barry lived by Marshfield Grove.

All five of them had been involved in lots of spooky moments. They'd formed the Zombie Hunters to talk about what they'd seen and heard. Sometimes they got together to check out ghosts or zombies.

Stan glanced out his window. He could see Hilltop Cemetery, which started at the edge of his yard. He knew he shouldn't go back out there. Not alone. Not at night.

But he couldn't resist.

Stan tied his sneakers and tiptoed down the stairs. He quietly opened the back door and stepped out. He didn't want his parents to know he was leaving.

Some leaves had fallen. They crunched under Stan's feet. He stopped walking and looked back. There was no sound from the house. So he moved slowly into the graveyard.

He climbed Deadman's Hill. The

Wyman and Fortin plots were on the next hill.

Stan gulped and kept walking. He had to circle through some deep woods to get to the Wyman area. He turned on his flashlight.

Stan jumped back. His light was shining on a man! The man was just ten feet away, but he wasn't looking at Stan. He was staring across the field at the Fortin graves.

"Hello," Stan said.

The man turned. His face looked very pale. His skin was stretched tight across his cheeks and jaw.

"Who are you?" he asked.

"Stan. Who are you?"

The man pointed toward the Fortin area. "Are you with them?"

Stan shook his head. "No. I'm alive." Stan took another step back. "Are you?"

The man laughed. Stan's light didn't seem to pass through him. But it was hard to tell in the dark.

"There's been no trouble here for many years," the man said. "Until tonight. The Fortins are at it again."

"At what?"

The man stooped down. He picked up a rock. He threw it across the graveyard, and it hit one of the Fortin gravestones.

Seconds later, something landed with a crash near the man's feet.

"They attack us for no reason," the man said. He cupped his hands around his mouth and shouted. "Stay off our land, Fortin!"

A shaky voice replied. "You stay off our land, Wyman!"

"It's our land!" the man shouted.

"No, it's not!"

Stan cleared his throat. The man turned to look at him.

"What land are you talking about?" Stan asked.

The man slowly swept his arm. "Right there," he said. "Our orchard. My family has taken care of this orchard for nearly 200 years. But the Fortins steal our apples. They trample our young trees."

Stan couldn't see the area because of the dark. But he knew that there was no orchard. The land between the Fortins and the Wymans was ragged old brush. There were a few scraggly trees, but they didn't produce apples.

Maybe it's a ghost orchard, Stan thought. The apples and the trees might not be any more solid than the ghosts. Maybe the ghosts could see the fruit, but Stan couldn't.

"You said that the Fortins have been quiet for years?" Stan asked.

"Until tonight," the man said. "They say we sent someone over to disturb their sleep. Then they attacked by throwing stones."

"It was me," Stan said. "I fell onto Randall's grave a few hours ago. He was mad about it. He chased me away."

"They are not tolerant people," the man said. "But they are clever. They've tricked us before."

"How did they trick you?"

The man glared at Stan. "Once they sent a boy about your age. He looked a lot like you. He said he'd come to make peace. We took the boy into our home. And while we were speaking to him, the other Fortins destroyed our orchard!"

"Did it grow back?" Stan asked.

"It took many years," the man said. "But yes, it's a wonderful orchard once again."

Stan shined his light toward the brushy area. "Right there?" he asked.

"Yes," said the man, "it's the finest orchard in the county."

Stan nodded. This man must be seeing something that wasn't there. He must be a ghost, too.

"Why would the Fortins want to ruin such a fine orchard?" Stan asked.

"Because they say the land is theirs."

"But it isn't?" Stan asked.

"It is not. It never has been. And it never will. It belongs to my family—the Wymans."

The man took two slow steps toward Stan. Stan took one step back.

"Any Fortin seen near our land will be dealt with harshly," the man said. "That will be your only warning."

"I'm not a Fortin," Stan said.

"You've been warned."

And then the man vanished. He didn't walk away. He didn't float off. He just disappeared.

Stan was shaking. He looked back toward his house. He couldn't see it. The night was too dark.

He looked toward the Wyman grave site. Then he looked toward Randall Fortin's.

He wasn't sure whose territory he was on. But he knew he wasn't safe.

So he walked as fast as he could toward home.

Stan's Journal: Thursday, September 24. 11:16 p.m.

I wonder when the last apple fell from a tree in the Wyman orchard. Probably early in the last century! I'm in that area all the time. I've never seen an apple. Or an apple tree. But two families of ghosts are at war over that orchard. And I've stirred up the latest battle by falling on someone's grave!

I'll get Jared out there with me tomorrow after school. And maybe the rest of the Zombie Hunters can check it out at night. Ghosts aren't usually dangerous. But those were real rocks they were throwing! Those families hate each other. And the cemetery will be a dangerous place until this ends.

Chapter 3:
A Big, Red Apple

The next afternoon, Stan and Jared climbed the hill to the old orchard.

"I don't see any apple trees," Jared said.

"I told you that," Stan said. "I've never seen an apple tree up here. And I've been coming to this graveyard since I was three years old."

In the daylight, Stan could see that there once had been some apple trees. A few wide stumps had rotted down to the ground. They must have been big trees many years before. Now the ground was thick with roots and rocks. Bramble bushes covered most of the site.

"Must have been a nice spot years ago," Jared said. He pointed to the dense pine trees that surrounded the area. "Very peaceful."

Jared stepped toward the fenced-in grave site. "Is that the Wyman area?" he asked.

"Yeah." Stan started to walk in that direction, too. "Let's take a closer look."

Stan had been scared last night, but he wasn't now. Having Jared along made him feel safer. And ghosts usually weren't active during the day.

"Check this out," Jared said, pointing to three gravestones in a row. "They all died on the same day."

"They did?"

"Yeah." Jared knelt in front of one of the stones. "September 24. Exactly 100 years ago yesterday! I wonder what happened."

Stan hadn't noticed the dates on the Wyman graves before. "Randall Fortin died on that same day!" he said. "He's the ghost who tried to scare me off last night."

He took a closer look at the stones. Frederick Wyman had been 58 years old. Thomas Wyman was 24. David Wyman had been 21.

"Looks like Frederick was their father," Jared said. "Maybe they died in an accident."

"Or maybe they were murdered," Stan said. "The Fortins and the Wymans hated each other. They might have had a deadly fight that day."

They looked at several other Wyman gravestones. They couldn't find any that were newer than those three. "These were the last of the Wymans," Stan said. "I wonder if Randall was the last of the Fortins, too?"

They checked the Fortins' graves next.

There were none that were more recent than Randall's. All of the other graves were from more than 100 years ago. Randall was the only one who had died on September 24.

"Some of these other graves go way back," Stan said. "My guess is that the Wymans and the Fortins were having a feud. Several men lost their lives because of it."

"All because of an apple orchard?" Jared asked.

"It looks that way," Stan said. "At least according to the ghosts I met. They said this land was the reason. Both sides think it's theirs."

"But why are they still fighting over it?" Jared asked. "It's been a century since they were alive."

"And it's not even an orchard anymore," Stan said. "I bet it's been fifty years since an apple grew here. Maybe longer."

Stan showed Jared the grave where he'd fallen the night before.

"What did you trip over?" Jared asked. "The ground looks smooth."

"It was dark," Stan said. "I thought I'd tripped over a root or a rock."

"Maybe the ghost tripped you," Jared said. He laughed. "He reached out of his grave and grabbed your ankle."

Stan frowned. "That might be true," he said. "The ghost was mean and angry."

Jared stamped his foot on Randall Fortin's grave.

"Don't do that," Stan said.

"Why not?" Jared said. "He can't hurt us." He jumped and landed hard on the grave.

"Let's come back tonight," Stan said. "I'll ask Amy to come with us."

"Sounds good," Jared said.

"There might not be any ghosts around," Stan said. "Last night was exactly 100 years after they died. They might rest for another hundred."

"Maybe," Jared said. "But if they're as angry as you say, then I don't think they'll be resting."

Jared headed for home. Stan stayed back for a few minutes. He looked at Randall Fortin's grave again. The ground was smooth. This spot seemed as peaceful as ever.

Stan set out for home. He went down the hill and started up the next one. And then he heard something hit the ground near him. It landed with a *thunk*.

Stan turned. And then he ducked. Something else was flying straight at him. It hit the grass and rolled away. Stan walked over to it. He gasped when he saw what it was.

It was a big, red apple.

Chapter 4:
Apple Toss

Stan's Journal: Friday, September 25. 6:38 p.m.

There are some angry ghosts in that graveyard! I can understand why they are mad at each other. But why are they mad at me? And which side is right? Who really owned that orchard? And why would anyone murder a neighbor because of it? Maybe we'll never know, but we'll try to find out. I pass through that cemetery every day. I don't want to have stones and apples thrown at me every time.

When Jared arrived, they went up to Stan's room and shut the door.

"Did you walk through the graveyards?" Stan asked.

Jared shook his head. "I came the long way."

"Scared?" Stan asked.

"No. Just careful."

Hillside Cemetery was connected to Woodland Cemetery by a path through the woods. Stan and Jared always went that way to each other's houses. It saved time and was usually very pleasant.

"Is Amy coming?" Jared asked.

"Yeah," Stan said. "I told her what was going on. We're supposed to be at her house by eight."

"What about Mitch and Barry?"

Stan drew in a breath. "I didn't tell them," he said. "They like to stir up trouble. I think this time we want to settle things down instead."

"Okay," Jared said. "But if we need help, we should get them."

"I plan to," Stan said. "If we need them. For now, let's try to keep this quiet."

Jared picked up a hammer from Stan's desk. "Do we need protection?"

"Hitting a ghost with a hammer won't do any good," Stan said. "It would pass right through it."

"What about those rocks they threw?"

Stan shrugged. "We just need to stay aware," he said. "I don't want to get hit with a rock. And somebody threw apples at me after you left this afternoon."

"We could wear football helmets," Jared said with a laugh.

Stan shook his head. "I'd rather not," he said. "But we'll be careful. Pay attention to every sound."

Stan and Jared made their way to Amy's house. As they walked, Stan thought about Mitch and Barry. They'd be angry that they hadn't been told about this. And it probably would be helpful to have them around. But Mitch and Barry would want to fight. Stan hoped to solve things without any battles this time.

"No weapons?" Amy asked as they headed into the graveyard.

Stan tapped his head with a finger. "Just our brains," he said.

Amy laughed. "That isn't saying much."

"I'm smarter than any ghost," Stan said. "We'll outsmart them. And maybe we can put an end to their feud."

"It's gone on for more than a century," Amy said. "What makes you think you can solve it in one night?"

"I don't know," Stan said. "But we'll give it a try."

"They might not be active tonight," Jared said. "Maybe they wake up only once every hundred years."

But that idea didn't last long. An apple came flying toward them. Stan heard it whizzing through the air. It plopped onto the hill beside them.

"They're active!" Stan said. He led Jared and Amy to a safer spot in the woods. They were about halfway between the two grave sites, but off to the side. They hunched down under a thick pine.

"These trees will block anything they throw," Stan said. "I hope!"

They could hear more apples landing near the grave sites. "Take that, Wyman!" came a shout.

"Back at you, Fortin!" came another.

"Is that all they do?" Amy whispered. "Throw apples at each other?"

"I don't think so," Stan said. He told her that at least four men had died on the same day up here. "Getting hit with an apple might sting. But it won't kill anyone."

"Then how did they die?" Amy asked.

"We don't know," Stan replied. "But when four men die on the same day, it means something. Especially when

they've been fighting over a piece of land."

Stan squinted and tried to see the ghosts. But it was very dark already. No ghosts were glowing.

The ground was soft here, covered in pine needles. Stan kneeled.

"Which side is friendly?" Amy asked. "The Fortins or the Wymans?"

"Neither," Stan said. "One of the Fortins warned me to stay away from them. But one of the Wymans said that any Fortin on their land would be killed. And he acted as if I was a Fortin!"

"So both sides are against us," Amy said.

Jared nodded, but Stan didn't agree. "Not exactly," he said. "The Fortins think I'm a Wyman. The Wymans think I'm a Fortin. We need to convince them that we aren't Wymans or Fortins."

"And you think they'll believe us?" Amy asked.

"Maybe," Stan said. "They hate each

other. But why would they hate us?"

"Because we're getting involved in this fight," Jared said. "If we just keep our noses out of it, we'll be left alone."

"Not true," Stan said. "I walk through this graveyard every day. More than once. Do you think I want to be ducking apples and rocks every time I come here?"

"I guess not," Jared said.

"So, we have to settle this feud," Stan said. "I don't know how. But we can start by talking to them. Somebody has to be reasonable, right?"

"Reasonable?" Jared said. "These are ghosts. And they're fighting over an orchard that hasn't produced an apple for a hundred years! How reasonable is that?"

"Keep your voice down," Stan said. "In their minds, the orchard is still there. And where do you think those apples are coming from?"

"A ghost orchard?" Amy asked.

"I think so," Stan said. "When I looked for the apple they threw at me this afternoon, I couldn't find it. It hit the ground right by my feet. I heard it and I saw it. But when I looked for it a moment later, it was gone."

"What about the rocks?" Jared asked.

"They were real," Stan said. "Rocks last forever. They don't turn into ghosts."

"But apples do?" Amy asked.

"Looks like it," Stan replied. He cupped his hand around an ear, trying to hear better. But there hadn't been any noise for a few minutes. "They stopped throwing things," he whispered.

"So what do we do now?" Amy asked.

Stan looked around. His eyes had adjusted to the dark, so he could see a little. They all had flashlights, but he didn't want to draw attention to them.

"Give it a few more minutes," Stan said. "Just to make sure they've stopped throwing apples."

"Tell me this," Jared said, "if they care so much about the orchard, then why are they wasting all those apples? They keep throwing them. They smash into glop when they hit. So nobody gets to keep the apples anyway."

Stan thought about that for a moment. But then he had something more important to consider. He could hear something moving slowly through the dry leaves. And it was coming straight toward their hiding spot!

Chapter 5:
The Glowing Tree

Amy grabbed Stan's arm. "What's that?" she said very quietly.

"Maybe just a squirrel," Stan whispered. "Or a bird."

"No," Amy said. She pointed toward the Wyman grave site. "That!"

Stan turned and saw a misty glow moving toward them. It seemed to be walking, but Stan couldn't see any legs or arms. Within a few seconds, it was right in front of them. But it kept moving.

"Hello?" Stan said with a shaky voice.

The ghostly form was like a fog. It was the size of a man, but it had no true shape. Stan looked hard for a face. He didn't see one.

The form drifted away. It stayed in the woods, but moved toward the Fortins' site. Soon it couldn't be seen at all.

Stan gulped. "That was definitely a ghost."

"Do you think it saw us?" Amy asked. "It didn't stop."

"I don't think it heard you," Jared said. "Or maybe it just ignored you."

Stan let out a deep breath. "That was weird," he said. "The ghosts I saw yesterday were in human form. They spoke to me. This one was very different."

"You're shaking," Amy said.

"This was scarier," Stan said. "I don't know why. I guess because I couldn't tell what it was thinking. Or what it might do. The other ones threatened me, but at least they acted human."

"And they looked human, right?" Jared asked.

"Yes," Stan said. "Randall Fortin was a ghost. You could see through him. The Wyman ghost looked solid, but he vanished into the air."

"That thing that just went past was really spooky," Amy said. "It acted like it didn't have a mind."

"I wonder if it was a Fortin or a Wyman," Stan said. "I'm sure it was one or the other."

And then he saw another ghost. This one was out in the area that had been the orchard. It looked like a boy, but Stan wasn't sure. He nudged Jared and pointed.

"I see it," Jared said. "In fact, I see more than one."

As they watched, several ghosts joined the first one. They appeared to be picking apples. They reached and pulled. But there were no trees to be seen.

These ghosts all had human form. They were mostly adults, and all were very white and misty. Stan didn't hear any sound, but it looked like they were talking to each other.

Stan pulled his small notebook out of his pocket. He began to write some notes.

Stan's Journal: Friday, September 25. About 9 p.m.

Five ghosts are visible. No sign of trouble. Looks like they're working in the orchard. Wish I could hear what they are saying.

"Let's go talk to them," Amy said.

"Are you crazy?" Jared asked.

"No," Amy replied. "They look harmless. They're just picking apples."

"You might be right," Stan said. "Maybe we're seeing a different time. Before the fighting. Maybe the Wymans and the Fortins are all tending the orchard together."

"What do you mean by 'a different time?'" Jared asked. "They're right there. Right now."

"Ghost time is weird," Stan said. "They get hung up on one event. They do the same thing over and over. So what we're seeing might have happened more than a hundred years ago."

"Then how could we talk to them?" Jared asked. "We're here now."

They watched the ghosts for several minutes. The ghosts seemed calm and happy.

"Let's try," Stan said. "It can't hurt to try to talk to them."

They stood up, but no one took a step.

"You go first," Amy said.

Stan shrugged. He walked carefully toward the orchard. And as he got closer, he began to see apple trees. They were very pale and did not look solid. But he could see their outlines. And they were loaded with apples.

"Hello," Stan said to the ghost who was nearest to him. But the boy didn't respond. He kept reaching for apples and putting them in a basket.

Stan tried again. "How are you?" he asked. But the ghost boy kept working. He was around Stan's age.

None of the other ghosts seemed to be aware of the Zombie Hunters.

Stan reached for an apple, but his hand passed right through! There was nothing to grab.

"Why are they picking apples at night?" Jared asked.

"This isn't real time," Stan said. "They can't see us or hear us. We can't touch the apples or the trees. All of what we're seeing happened a long time ago. It's probably daytime in their world."

"Very strange," Jared said. He turned toward an older ghost who was carrying a basket of apples. "Hey!" Jared said. "Over here. Can you hear me?"

The ghost ignored Jared. He kept walking toward the Wyman property.

"They don't know we are here," Stan said. "We're like ghosts to them. The same way they are to us."

"But we can see them," Jared said. "Why can't they see us?"

Stan thought about that for a moment. "That's probably because what they're doing already happened," he said. "A century ago. But back then, we hadn't happened yet. We're seeing back in time. But they can't see forward to our time."

"Makes sense, I guess," Jared said.

Stan noticed that one of the apple trees was glowing much brighter than the others. "Look at that," he said. "I wonder what's going on."

The tree was the largest one. Its trunk was wide and its branches were high. It was loaded with fruit. Stan headed toward it.

"Be careful," Jared said. "It might be radioactive or something."

"I doubt it," Stan said. "It probably just has more ghostly energy because it's older."

But as he got closer, Stan felt himself being pulled. The tree's energy was like a magnet. Stan was moving quickly toward the trunk. He put up his hands to stop himself. But the tree sucked him in.

The air was suddenly very cold. Stan was falling. There was a bright flash of light, and then everything was dark. He heard a squishing sound, and he landed in a heap on the ground.

Stan looked around. It was daylight already. He was at the base of a large apple tree in an orchard at the top of a hill.

He was in the same spot. But it wasn't the same at all!

Chapter 6:
Back in Time

"Amy?" Stan called. "Jared?"

The other Zombie Hunters were gone. Stan was in the orchard alone. The trees were healthy and strong. They were loaded with apples.

Across the way, Stan could see a white house near the Wymans' grave site. There were gravestones, but not as many as before. And where had that house come from?

On the other side of the orchard was another house. It was back where the

Fortins were buried. There was a family burial plot there, too.

Stan picked an apple from a tree. It was solid. He bit into it, and juice ran down his chin. The apple tasted sweet and tart at the same time. Better than any apple he'd ever eaten.

No one was around. The sun was low in the sky, so it seemed to be early morning. He walked quietly toward the Wyman graves and read a few.

PATRICK WYMAN
At rest

LUCILLE WYMAN BAKER
At peace

JACOB WYMAN
Called to Heaven

He'd read those same stones just

yesterday. But now the stones looked new. They weren't 100 years old anymore.

I've gone back in time, Stan thought. He felt his arms and his stomach. He wasn't a ghost. He was as solid as ever.

The dirt path he usually walked along was wider now. But the woods all around were dense. This didn't seem to be a public cemetery yet. There were just three clearings. One for the orchard. One for the Wymans' home. And one for the Fortins'.

What about my house? Stan wondered. *How old was that house? About a hundred years,* he thought. He headed across Deadman's Hill to see.

The house was there. But it was painted white with dark-green trim. It looked brand new. The house had been gray with white trim for all of Stan's life.

There were only a few other houses on the street. And the street was a dirt road! It had always been paved.

Stan did not go any farther. He headed for the apple trees. He'd been thrown back in time through the orchard. Maybe he could return the same way.

Someone was coming toward him. It looked like the ghost boy he'd seen picking apples. But he didn't look like a ghost anymore. He was as solid as Stan.

"Hello," the boy said. "Are you new around here?"

"That's our house over there," Stan said. He waved his hand in that direction. "Down the hill."

"The new house?" the boy asked. "I didn't know that the family had a child as old as you. Are you a cousin?"

"Something like that," Stan said. "I'm Stan. Where do you live?"

"Right there," Josh said. He pointed to the Fortins' house.

"Oh," Stan said. "I thought you were a Wyman."

Josh's face grew dark. He scowled. "That's the worst thing I could ever be," he said. "I'm Josh Fortin. The Wymans are crooks. They steal our apples."

"From the orchard?" Stan asked.

"Of course," Josh said. "We tend that orchard very carefully. But every fall, the Wymans steal apples. They do it at night, thinking that we won't know. But they take too many."

"Why don't they just buy some from you?" Stan asked. "Or trade?"

"Because they are thieves," Josh replied. "Our families used to get along very well. We're the only ones who live on this hill. We once worked together, and were good neighbors. But the latest generation of Wymans are bad seeds. They are lazy. They steal."

"So, your families used to get along?" Stan asked.

"Of course," Josh said. "We're two

of the oldest families in Marshfield. My great-grandparents settled this hill. The Wymans were their good friends."

"And how long have the families been fighting?"

"A few years," Josh said. "The bad feelings started even before that."

"Why did they start stealing?" Stan asked.

Josh shrugged. "I don't know. They say the orchard belongs to them. But it's been my family's land for many years."

Stan kicked at some dry leaves. The air was warm, but the grass and the surrounding brush were brown. "Looks like we need rain," Stan said.

"It hasn't rained in three months," Josh said. "The apple trees have deep roots, so they seem all right. But we do need a good soaking here."

Stan bent and felt the grass. It was brittle from the heat.

"I must be getting to school now," Josh said. "Have you enrolled yet?"

"Not yet," Stan said.

"You'd best be enrolling soon," Josh said. "Do it before the truant officer finds that you are missing."

"Maybe tomorrow," Stan said.

Josh left for school. Stan didn't know what to do. He sat on a rock and looked around. The sky was a deep blue. The air smelled crisp. Was the air really cleaner a hundred years ago?

The woods looked a little different, too. There were more leafy trees, and fewer pines. The leaves had just begun to change colors, with hints of red and yellow and orange.

Stan looked down and noticed a small notebook sitting in the leaves. Had Josh dropped it? He might need it for school.

"Hey, Josh!" Stan called. But Josh was nowhere near.

Stan opened the notebook. It was filled with short notes, all of them dated.

It's a diary, Stan thought. *Just like mine.*

He'd return it to Josh later. But the diary might offer some clues to the fight between the Wymans and the Fortins.

And maybe it would help Stan figure out how to get home.

Chapter 7:
Nothing to Lose

S tan opened Josh's diary and began to read. He felt guilty about snooping in someone else's private thoughts, but this was too important. Stan had gone back in time by a hundred years. This diary might help him escape.

September 20

    The apples are nearly ripe. So far there has been little bickering this year. But I know there will be fighting soon. For several years, there has been much stress about who owns the apples. Father says our families

*used to share the fruit. But then the
Wymans said it all belonged to them.
Father says all of the apples really
belong to us. Our family planted the
trees many years ago.*

Stan looked at the date. Josh had written those words almost exactly 100 years before. That meant Randall Fortin and the three Wymans were still alive. But they'd soon be dead.

Randall must be Josh's father, Stan thought. He tried to remember if he'd ever seen a gravestone for Josh Fortin. He didn't think so. But why not? Josh would be at least 112 by now, and most likely dead. But he wasn't buried at the Fortin grave site.

Stan turned the page and continued to read. He had to find out what happened.

*September 21
    David Wyman made a threat
today. He told me if we took any*

apples this year, there would be big trouble. He wouldn't say what would be done. But he implied that it would be severe. I told Father. He said what he always says, "The apples belong to us." But he also said he'd do whatever he had to do to battle the Wymans.

Stan let out a low whistle. He could see the trouble brewing. It was hard to believe that families would be willing to fight so hard over apples.

He looked around. No one was stirring at either house. Stan wasn't ready to talk to the Wymans or the Fortins yet. So he stayed in the woods.

He needed more information.

September 22

We picked our first bushel of apples today. Father insisted that we go to the orchard before sunup. There was very little light, but we picked fast. I asked him why we were being so secretive. He said he had other work to do today, and wanted to pick early. But I'm sure he was trying to avoid the Wymans. Perhaps that's a good idea. Why stir up trouble?

Stan still had no idea which family was right. Maybe neither side was. If they had shared the orchard for so many years, why couldn't they do it now? Someone must have become very greedy. Maybe both sides had.

September 23

David and Thomas Wyman stole our apples last night. They walked right into our home and took the bushel. But first they punched Father! And David shoved me into a wall. They warned us to stay out of the orchard.

Father shouted that it was our orchard. He said that our family had always allowed the Wymans to take as many apples as they wanted. And he told them they were not welcome in the orchard anymore.

The Wymans laughed and said they'd beat Father and me if we set foot near the apple trees. Father said they'd be sorry.

There was only one more diary entry.

September 24

I saw a boy about my age take an apple from the orchard. He is a stranger to me. Perhaps he is a Wyman cousin. I will go see what he is up to. The Wymans may be bringing more family members here for a fight. He might be one of them.

That's me, Stan thought. *Josh had written that note this morning. So today was September 24. The day that Randall Fortin and the three Wymans had died!*

Stan had gone back in time by 100 years, plus one day. *How strange,* he thought.

Something bad was going to happen tonight. Could Stan prevent it? Could he

save four lives? Would that somehow help
him get back to his real life?

Stan closed the diary. He'd return it to
Josh later. When he looked up, he saw two
young men standing in the field next to the
Wyman house.

Stan figured that they must be David
and Thomas Wyman. He took a deep

breath and let it out. Before he had thought things through, he was walking toward the Wymans.

He had nothing to lose. Or did he?

Chapter 8:
A Warning

The Wymans were staring at Stan as he approached. Stan gulped. They looked mean. He didn't know what he would say.

"Can we help you?" the younger man said. Stan figured that must be David. He didn't sound friendly at all.

"I'm just passing through," Stan said. "I was on my way to town."

"Well, keep moving," said the other Wyman. "This is private land."

"I don't mean any harm," Stan said. "I

was wondering if you could spare a glass of water. I'm thirsty."

David Wyman frowned. He pointed toward a well. "There's water," he said. "Help yourself."

Stan looked down the well. It was round, with deep stone walls. A bucket on a crank went down to the water. Stan had seen old wells like this in movies, but he'd never tried to use one. The water smelled stale and musty.

"Could I have an apple instead?" Stan asked. "That would quench my thirst and ease my hunger."

Thomas Wyman folded his arms across his chest. "I think you've already had some of those apples," he said. "Someone took a bushel or two last night."

"It wasn't me," Stan said. He knew from Josh's diary that the Fortins had taken some. And that the Wymans had taken them back!

David Wyman stepped closer to Stan and gave him a light shove. "Those are our apples, Fortin. Keep away from them."

"I'm not a Fortin," Stan said.

"We saw you talking to Josh this morning," David said. "You can't fool us."

"I did talk to Josh," Stan said. "But I'm not a Fortin. And I didn't steal any apples."

David pushed Stan again.

"Let him be," Thomas said. "This boy says he isn't a Fortin. He says he's just passing through."

Thomas turned to Stan. "So be on your way. Take one apple, if you'd like. But if we see you with the Fortins again, we'll know that you are a liar. And you'll suffer, as they will."

Stan stayed put. "Josh said your families used to share the apples," he said. "Why can't you do that now?"

"Because the orchard is ours!" Thomas said. "It's true that our families used to share the fruit. But the orchard has always belonged to us. When the Fortins began to take too many apples, we asked them to be fair. But they started stealing the apples in the night."

"And then we put a stop to it," David said. "The Fortins are thieves. And we will protect our orchard from them in any way we need to."

Stan nodded. He didn't believe that the Wymans owned the orchard. But he could tell that they were serious. They'd beat him up or worse if he stayed here.

"Thank you for the apple," Stan said. He picked a nice round one and headed along the path.

"Just keep moving," Thomas said. "And don't come back here if you know what's good for you."

What a couple of creeps, Stan thought. He wasn't sure what was true. It seemed clear that the two families had once shared the orchard. But both sides claimed to own it.

He'd been warned to stay away. But Stan knew that his only way back "home" was through that orchard. He'd stay away until Josh returned. But he would definitely be back soon.

The thought of dealing with the Wymans gave him a shudder. They'd beat him up or try to kill him if they saw him with Josh Fortin.

But then another thought crossed Stan's mind. If those gravestones were correct, then David and Thomas were going to die tonight. Their father was, too. And so was Randall Fortin.

Maybe I can stop that, Stan thought. *Or maybe this is my night to die, too!*

Chapter 9:
The Fortins

Stan's Journal: September 24 (I think). Around noon. 100 years ago!

I'm starving. Two apples just isn't enough. I need to find some food so I'll have enough strength for tonight. I don't even know what will happen tonight, but I know it won't be fun. This is the night four men become ghosts. Or maybe five us of! Imagine that. I'd have to wait 100 years to see Jared and Amy and my parents again. And I'd be a century-old ghost by then. Still caught in a century-old feud over an apple orchard!

Stan had made his way down the hill and over toward Jared's house. But Jared's house wasn't there. The area was mostly thick forest.

Woodland Cemetery was there, but it was much smaller than Stan remembered. On the edge of the cleared area Stan saw what looked like berries. He hurried over.

It was a grape vine. The bunches of deep-blue grapes smelled sweet. Stan broke off a branch and plucked a single grape off the stem. He popped the grape in his mouth.

The first bite took him by surprise. The green flesh was sour, and it was loaded with big pits. But the purple flesh just below the skin was much sweeter. He chewed until all that was left was the tough skin. He spit it out and ate several more. He wiped his blue-stained fingers on his shirt.

Stan sat on the grassy hill by some gravestones. He could see the town of Marshfield down below. Many of the buildings were the same, but there were not nearly as many. There were fewer streets, too.

Stan yawned. He tried to figure out what time it would be if he was back in his own year. It had been after nine o'clock at night when he fell through the glowing tree. And when he landed, it seemed to be about seven o'clock in the morning. So he'd been awake for a long time.

The grass was soft but very dry. Stan lay down and shut his eyes. He needed to rest for tonight. He didn't mean to fall asleep, but he did.

In his dream, Stan was being chased. The night was dark. He didn't know who was chasing him, but he could hear them getting closer. Stan was carrying an armload of apples.

He ran down a hill and came to a river. The water was moving very fast. White waves crashed and the wind howled. On this side of the river, everything was dark, misty, and cold.

The other side of the river looked bright and sunny. Stan could see his house. It was painted gray again, and all of the other homes were there, too. The street was paved. Stan could see his parents and his friends.

He tried to yell, but no sound came out. He could hear the people who were chasing him. They were very close. They had mean, barking dogs that were snarling. They would reach him in a few seconds.

Stan's only way to escape was to plunge into the river. He might drown, but perhaps he could swim to safety.

He turned and saw all of the Wymans and Fortins running toward him. They were swinging clubs and shouting.

Stan leaped into the river. And then he shook himself awake.

He was sweating, and he was gasping for

breath. His heart was racing. But he was safe. He was on dry land in the cemetery.

He looked around but saw no one.

Was he really safe? *I'm still stuck in the past,* he thought. *Not safe at all.*

Stan had no idea how long he had slept. It seemed to be quite a bit later in the day— perhaps midafternoon. His stomach was grumbling with hunger.

Then he heard a voice.

"Stan?"

It was Josh. He looked puzzled as he walked toward Stan.

"What are you doing here?" Josh asked.

"I was resting," Stan said. He knew that he should return Josh's diary. And that he must warn him about what might happen tonight.

"I found this after you left this morning," Stan said. He handed the diary to Josh.

"Thanks," Josh said. "Did you read it?"

Stan looked away. "I glanced at it," he

said. "I'm sorry."

"It's all right," Josh said. "It's not very personal."

Stan needed to make sure of the date. "Today is September 24, right?" he asked.

"Yes," Josh replied. "Why?"

Stan thought for a minute. "This is hard to explain," he said. "But I believe this fight between your family and the Wymans will end badly. And the worst of it will happen tonight."

Josh narrowed his eyes. "Why do you say that?" he demanded.

"You would not believe me," Stan said. "But I think I know the future."

"Nonsense," Josh said.

Stan shook his head. "According to your diary, the situation is very tense. I spoke to the Wymans earlier today. They are prepared for a big fight."

"So are we," Josh said. "But this has gone on for some time."

"Tonight will be the worst," Stan said.

"You said that already."

"Because it's true!"

Josh stared at Stan. "Let's talk to Father," he said. "He'll know what to do. But he won't believe that you can see the future!"

"That's not exactly what I'm doing," Stan said. "I'm really seeing the past."

"But you said you knew what would happen tonight," Josh said as they walked.

"Right," Stan replied. "Like I said, it's hard to explain."

They'll think I'm nuts if I tell them the truth, Stan thought. *I see the future because it already happened? Even I find that hard to believe.*

Josh's father introduced himself as Randall Fortin. Stan didn't tell him that they'd met before.

"I'm glad to meet a new neighbor," Randall said. "Our old neighbors have been nothing but trouble."

"I know," Stan said. "I'm afraid that the trouble will be even worse tonight."

"Why do you say that?" Randall asked. "Have you spoken to the Wymans?"

"I did," Stan said. "They said you will suffer. And they said I will suffer, too, if they see me with you."

Randall nodded. They were standing in the yard in front of the house. "We are not afraid of the Wymans," he said. "But we must be careful. They are stubborn and dangerous. And they think they own the orchard. They do not."

"Would it help for you to talk to them?" Stan asked.

Randall snorted. "We've tried many times," he said. "They never listen. Now they've become violent. They attacked Josh and me last night. Took a bushel of apples. And they threatened us."

"Are any of them reasonable?" Stan asked.

Randall shrugged. "The father used to be," he said. "But his sons have bullied him, too. Now he acts like they do."

"Did you used to be friends?" Stan asked.

"Yes," Randall said. "Frederick Wyman used to be a good neighbor. But those days are over."

Stan looked across the orchard at the Wyman house. David and Thomas were watching. Stan gulped. They'd warned him to stay away from the Fortins.

"Is it all right if we go inside?" Stan asked. "I could use a glass of water."

He glanced back. Both of the Wymans had their arms folded. They were staring at Stan and the Fortins. They looked like they were ready for trouble.

"Let's go in the back way," Josh said. He led Stan through the yard. After his father had gone in, Josh took the diary from his pocket. He placed it in a small metal box behind one of the gravestones. Then he covered it with a rock.

"I don't want Father to read my diary," Josh said. "So I hide it out here by my grandfather's grave."

The Fortins' house was small. They sat in the kitchen at a wooden table. Randall offered Stan some bread and cheese.

"Thank you," Stan said. "I haven't had any lunch."

There was one cow and several sheep in a fenced area behind the house.

"How many Fortins live here?" Stan asked.

"Just two of us," Josh said. "My uncles live nearby with their families. My mother died several years ago."

"There have been many Fortins on this land," Randall said. "But now it's just us two."

Stan wondered what would happen to Josh if Randall died tonight. Josh would be the only one left on this hill. What had Josh done after his father died? Had he stayed in Marshfield? Why wasn't he buried near his father?

"I'd like to meet your parents," Randall said.

"Yes," Stan said. "So would I."

"Pardon?"

Stan blushed. "I mean, I should be getting home soon."

"I'm wondering something," Randall said. "You seem to be a fine boy. Perhaps you could speak to Frederick Wyman. I'd like to settle this feud in a reasonable manner. But they get violent whenever I approach them."

Stan let out his breath. "They threatened me, too. Told me to stay away from them. And from you."

"That was David and Thomas," Josh said. "Not Frederick."

Stan shook his head. And then he

jumped from his chair as a glass window shattered.

"Yikes!" Stan said. A large stone had crashed through the window.

"Those Wymans!" Josh said. "They never stop!"

"They're terrible people," Randall said.

A shout came from across the way. "Take that as a warning, Fortin! Stay away from our orchard!"

"We'll do no such thing!" Randall yelled back. "It's our orchard. You stay away."

"Is there a sheriff around here?" Stan asked. "Someone who can control those people?"

"We can handle this without the law," Randall said. "We're in the right. We will protect our orchard alone."

Stan could hear the Wymans laughing.

Randall looked very angry, but he didn't do anything about it.

He's waiting for dark, Stan thought. *He thinks he can handle this. If he only knew!*

"You could die tonight!" Stan said.

Randall shook his head. "The Wymans are mean, but they are not murderers," he said. "Nor are we."

That's what you think, Stan thought. Four men were going to die tonight. He didn't know how. Maybe it would be an accident. Maybe it would be murder.

But, maybe Stan could keep it from happening. If only he had an idea how.

"I'll be going now," Stan said. "Perhaps I'll see you again later."

Josh was sweeping up the broken glass. "Think about what Father asked you," he said. "If you were to speak to Frederick Wyman, we might be able to resolve this."

"But his sons are hotheads," Stan said. "They want to hurt us all."

"Think it over," Josh said. "You say that you can see the future. Maybe you can *change* the future, too."

"I hope so," Stan said softly. "But I don't know if talking to the Wymans is the way."

The only thing that might change is one more death, Stan thought. *Mine!*

Chapter 10:
Ghosts of the Future

Stan carefully stepped out of the house, looking for the Wymans. They weren't around.

Good, he thought. He wasn't ready to face them yet.

He made his way around the back of the house. Then he crossed through the woods. He needed to do a lot of thinking. He needed a plan. And he needed to stay out of sight.

Stan headed back toward Jared's house. Of course he knew that there was no house there. But he felt safe in that area. He knew the land, and it was far enough away from the Wymans.

He sat in the grass again, right where he'd been before. He'd filled up on bread and cheese, so he felt better. He took out his notebook to write.

Stan's Journal: September 24. Early evening.

Frederick Wyman is probably the ghost I spoke to the first night. The one who said he could see the orchard, even though it had been gone for 100 years!

He was mean. Just like his sons. And he warned me to stay away. I'd be taking a big chance if I went over there. David and Thomas saw me with Josh again. Now they're sure that I'm a Fortin.

Stan set down his pen. What if he never returned to the present day? He wasn't supposed to be born for another eighty-eight years. By then he'd be 100 years old!

He was on his own. He had no idea how to get back. And he was scared.

I guess I don't have much to lose. Should I save four lives if it means that I have to stay here forever? Or should I try to get back right now? So what if Randall and the Wymans die tonight? They were going to die anyway. At least I'll be back to normal.

But saving them might be my only way back. I have no other plan. At least if I save Randall, I'll know an adult here. Maybe I can move in with him and Josh. I have nowhere else to go.

Stan felt very sad. He missed his mom and his dad. He missed Jared, Amy, and the other Zombie Hunters. They'd helped him out of many jams before. But he couldn't reach them now. They were a hundred years away.

He lay back again. He didn't sleep, but he stayed still for a long time. He thought about his life. He wanted it back to normal.

A movement grabbed Stan's attention. A deer had stepped out of the forest. It was eating grass nearby. Stan watched for a few minutes, staying as still as he could.

The deer seemed to smell him. It lifted its head and stared in his direction. Then it turned and trotted back into the woods.

I'll try to speak to Frederick Wyman. But what should I say? That the Fortins want to end the fight? What would that solve? Both sides are sure that they own the orchard. Would they agree to share it again? I doubt it.

What if the Wymans are right? Randall and Josh seem like nice people, but maybe they're lying. Or maybe Josh just doesn't know any better. He would believe whatever his father says. I think the Wymans are lying. But from what I've seen of Randall Fortin, he can be mean, too. He was bitter when he yelled at me a few nights ago.

But then again, he'd been dead for 100 years by then.

The sun was already setting. It would be dark in a little while. If Stan was going to talk to anyone, it would have to be soon. He had no idea what time Randall and the Wymans were going to die. But it would have to be before midnight. Their gravestones said they'd died today.

Can I change the past? Can I stop four deaths that happened so long ago? And what happens if I do? Will the orchard stay healthy? Will it still have trees 100 years from now?

And will I be buried in Hilltop Cemetery by then? Maybe Amy and Jared and the others will trip over my grave some day. Maybe I'll be haunting them! I'll be a ghost who can never rest, because I missed out on my real life. I had to live it a century earlier than I was supposed to. I had to grow up now!

Another movement caught Stan's eye. Two figures were coming toward him on the path.

He huddled lower to the ground. He did not want to be seen.

Stan couldn't hear any voices. But he could see the figures clearly. They were pale and misty. More ghosts.

Stan's mouth went dry. His skin felt cold and clammy These weren't just scary ghosts. He knew those people.

The ghosts were Amy and Jared!

"Over here!" Stan said. He waved his arms. But the ghosts didn't see him. They kept walking.

"Amy!" Stan yelled. He ran right up to her. "Jared!"

But there was no response.

Now I'm seeing the future, Stan thought. *They're 100 years ahead of me.*

But that didn't seem right either. They were here. And they seemed alive. The past and the future were overlapping.

Maybe he could follow Jared and Amy back to his real time. And maybe they could help him.

He'd have to figure out how to communicate with them.

It was dark now. Stan could barely see his friends. He walked behind them. They were heading toward the orchard.

I think they're really here, Stan thought. They'd come to help. But since they were in a different time, they couldn't see him. Not yet.

That orchard has a lot of ghostly energy, Stan thought. It was how he'd been thrown back in time.

So it had to hold the key for throwing him forward.

At least he hoped that was true.

Chapter 11:
Negotiator Stan

Before long, Stan had lost track of Jared and Amy. He'd never felt more alone in his life. He sat on a bale of hay in the Fortins' yard and tried to summon his courage.

Tonight may be my only chance to get home, Stan thought. The ghostly energy would be very strong tonight. He had to use that energy to help him get home. But how?

Everything was dark. There were no electric lights up here. Stan could see candles flickering inside the house.

He jumped when something wet and warm nudged his cheek. The cow!

"Hey," Stan said softly. "It's all right."

The cow stared at him. Stan walked to the door and knocked.

"What have you decided?" Josh asked as Stan entered the house. The kitchen window had been boarded over.

"I'll try to talk to the Wymans," Stan replied. "What do you think I should say?"

"Tell them it is our orchard," Randall said. "We're willing to share the apples again. But fairly."

"They say the orchard is theirs," Stan said.

"They are wrong."

"I know that," Stan said. "But they don't think so. I don't see how they'll agree to share the apples unless you'll share the ownership."

"But we own the orchard," Randall said.

Stan sighed. He was getting nowhere.

"Just speak to them for a few minutes," Randall said. "Keep their attention. Josh and I will be along shortly."

Keep their attention? What did Randall mean by that? "Why will you be along?" Stan asked.

"You speak to them first," Randall said. "After they see that you are sincere, we'll come. Then we can discuss the matter."

"What if they won't listen to me?"

"They will," Randall said. "Keep them occupied for ten minutes. Tell them we are willing to share the apples."

"But only if they agree that you own the orchard?" Stan asked.

"We do own the orchard," Randall said sharply. "The Wymans know that is a fact."

Stan looked away.

"You should go now," Randall said.

Stan nodded. "What if they say no?"

Randall smiled. "We will be along in

ten minutes. Be sure to go into their house. Talk to them. Keep them busy."

This was sounding very strange. What did Randall have planned? If he was going to attack the Wymans, then Stan didn't want to be there.

"Are you setting me up?" Stan asked.

"I don't know what you mean," Randall said.

"Are you planning to attack the Wymans while I'm there? When I'm 'keeping them busy?'" Stan asked.

This time Randall laughed. "We want only to make peace with our neighbors," he said. "Explain things to them, please."

Randall grabbed Stan's arm and led him to the door. "We need your help to end this feud," he said. "Go now."

Before he knew it, Stan was outside. The door was shut behind him.

He waited for his eyes to adjust to the darkness. He could see the Wymans' house across the way. Candles were burning there, too. But everything between the two houses was dark. Stan walked carefully.

Stan wondered if the other Zombie Hunters were watching him. He couldn't see them. But, he knew that if they were around, they would do everything they could to help.

He stared at the Wymans' side door for several minutes before he finally knocked. The door swung open quickly.

"What do you want, Fortin?" David Wyman asked.

Stan gulped. "I'm not a Fortin," he said. "But I am a friend. I'd like to speak to you."

"We don't want anything to do with a Fortin or one of their friends," David said. He began to shut the door.

"Hold on," came a voice from within.

The door opened again. Frederick Wyman had pushed David aside. Stan could see that Thomas was there, too.

"May I come in?" Stan asked.

"What is it you want?" Frederick replied.

"I was hoping to talk to you about the orchard," Stan said. "Things are getting too heated between you and the Fortins. They seem to want to make amends. Isn't there some way to share the apples fairly?"

Frederick scowled. But he stepped aside and told Stan to come in.

The room was very dark, with just one small candle burning. David and Thomas sat at a table. Frederick leaned against the wall with his arms folded.

"Randall Fortin is nasty," Frederick said. "He claims to own the orchard. But he steals the apples in the dark! If he owned the orchard, why would he be so sneaky?"

"I don't know," Stan said. "He says his family has owned the orchard for many years."

"It is hard to believe anything he says,"

Frederick said. "But he seems to have fooled you. And he fooled his son."

"If Randall is so sincere about making amends, then why isn't he here?" David demanded. "Why does he send a boy we don't even know? He needs to talk to us man-to-man."

All three Wymans stood up. They glared at Stan.

"Go tell that coward to come see us when he wants to talk," Frederick said. "It's our orchard and those are our apples. When he's ready to admit that, then maybe we can have a discussion."

Stan stumbled as he left the house. He fell again, but landed in a pile of dry leaves. They crinkled as he got to his feet.

He was shaking. The Wymans were mean people. But they might be right. One of the families must own the orchard. It might as well be them instead of the Fortins.

He could see a small light on the other side of the orchard. It was a candle.

"Hello?" Stan said as he got closer.

Randall held up the candle so Stan could see his face. "Did you make any progress?" he asked.

Stan shook his head. He told Randall and Josh what the Wymans had said.

Randall turned to Josh. "Go back to the house and get another candle," he said.

Randall waited until Josh was gone. "Tell them I agree," he said to Stan. "Go tell the Wymans that I know they own the orchard. I hope they'll agree to let us have our share of apples."

Stan couldn't believe what he was hearing. Randall obviously did not want Josh to hear this. But why the change?

"This fight has gone on too long," Randall said. "I'm ending it tonight. Now go back to them. I'll be along in ten minutes."

Stan started to protest, but Randall was firm.

"Go!" he said. "Tell them ten minutes."

Stan sighed. He didn't know what Randall was up to, but it didn't seem good. There was no way he would give up the orchard so easily. But he had admitted that the Wymans owned it. Or was he playing some kind of trick?

As Stan walked back to the Wymans, he noticed a very soft glow in the woods. He could not make out any features. But he did think the glow was aware of him.

Was it Amy and Jared? Stan hoped so. He felt a little less afraid just knowing that they might be there.

The door opened before Stan had a chance to knock.

"Where is he?" Frederick said.

"Who?"

"Fortin!"

"He'll be along soon," Stan said. "But

he admitted that you own the orchard."

Frederick spit into the yard. "He's not to be trusted," he said. "But we'll listen to him."

"He's a fool and a liar," David said.

Thomas laughed. "Some would say that we are, too."

"We have the deed to that orchard," Frederick said. "I'll show it to you. Just so you'll know for sure."

"You'll see that your friend does not tell the truth," David said.

While Frederick searched for the deed, Stan sat at the table with David and Thomas. He noticed that David was missing two fingers on his left hand. Thomas had a scar that went from the corner of his mouth to his eye. And both Wyman brothers smelled awful.

When Frederick returned, he said that he could not find the deed. "But we do own the orchard," he said. "We have proof."

"We just can't find it," David said.

Stan nodded. He didn't think anyone was telling him the truth anymore.

"So where is he?" Frederick said. "I suppose he's too afraid to come here after all. Perhaps we should go see him instead."

"Give him a few more minutes," Stan said. "He said he would come."

All three Wymans stared at Stan. He felt very uncomfortable. Would they beat him up if Randall didn't show? Or would they let him go?

"Nice house you have here," Stan said.

The Wymans didn't speak.

"Nice orchard, too," Stan said. He was starting to sweat again.

He turned to look out the window. He could see a glow, bigger than before. It must be the Zombie Hunters. He felt at ease right away. But then he realized what the glow really was. He could see it and smell it.

It was a fire.

The orchard was going up in flames!

Chapter 12:
Fire!

"You tricked us!" David yelled as he jumped up. "You distracted us so they could light the orchard on fire."

"No, I didn't," Stan said. "I had no idea."

"We'll deal with you later," Frederick said. He was rushing out the door. "Get water and shovels! We need to save the orchard."

Because the grass and the leaves were so dry, the fire spread quickly. Some of the apple trees had already caught fire.

Stan could feel the heat. He could see

Josh and Randall shoveling dirt onto the fire across the way. David and Thomas rushed over with their shovels and beat at the flames. Frederick brought a bucket of water, but it wasn't nearly enough.

"Dig a trench!" Randall said. "We have to stop it from spreading."

Everyone started digging, but the flames drove them back. They managed to dig a ditch that stopped the flames, but the fire simply spread the other way.

Stan shoveled as quickly as he could. He felt terrible about the fire. He had tried to warn everyone that tonight would be a bad one, but he hadn't known why. He should have been more forceful.

This fire might kill us all, Stan thought. *I have to be careful. So do they!*

"Why did you do this?" David shouted to Randall. "Now none of us will have an orchard!"

"It was an accident," Randall said. "I

dropped my candle. The fire spread quickly."

"You are lying!" Thomas said. "You set this fire on purpose. You did it because you know we are the rightful owners."

"Be quiet, all of you!" Frederick said. "Save the orchard first."

Stan threw more dirt on the flames.

"You're a fool, Fortin!" David said. "A dangerous fool."

"It was a mistake," Randall said.

"I said be quiet!" Frederick yelled again.

They seemed to be making some progress. The fire was mostly in a smaller area now. They kept throwing dirt at it.

But then a flaming branch fell from one of the trees. It landed on the other side of the ditch. Flames shot up there, too. Now there were two fires.

Stan and Josh turned to the new fire and began to shovel dirt on it. The others stayed with the original flames. But both fires grew rapidly.

"We're trapped!' David yelled.

The fires had surrounded them. Stan coughed from the smoke. His eyes stung badly.

"Faster!" Fredrick called.

They worked even harder. Stan's arms were aching from the strain. But he kept shoveling. He and Josh put out part of the fire. But it was spreading faster than they could work.

I don't want to die, Stan thought. But this was it. He was in the middle of the fatal fire. The one that had killed Randall and the three Wymans. Had Josh died, too? Why was there no gravestone for him? Maybe he'd been burned so badly that there'd been nothing left to bury.

The flames were so high that the entire orchard was glowing. There wasn't much land that wasn't on fire. All six people were backed into an area no bigger than

a garage. Everything around them was ablaze. There was no way out.

But Stan saw an even brighter glow. The largest tree in the orchard was shining with light. It was the tree Stan had fallen into when he first went back in time. It might be his only way out.

Stan dropped his shovel, "Follow me!" he yelled. He ran toward the tree. The others came with him.

Stan felt the same pull as before. He was sucked into the tree, and he fell into a cool, empty space. It was a huge relief after all that heat.

He landed with a thud and found himself sitting in the dark on hard ground. He was dizzy. He felt his chest and legs. He was solid. Was he back in real time?

"Stan?" a voice asked. "Where have you been?" It was Amy.

"I'm not sure," Stan said. "How long have I been gone?"

"About half an hour," Jared said. "We've been looking all over for you."

Half an hour? Stan thought. *It had been a whole day! Where had the time really gone?*

"Give me your light," he said to Jared. He clicked it on and shined it all around. There were no apple trees. Everything looked the same as before.

Stan was thrilled to be alive. But what about the others? They had to have died in the fire. There had been no way to escape.

Stan shook his head. The only way out of those flames had been through that glowing apple tree. But he was the only one who got there.

That meant Josh must have died, too.

Chapter 13:
Back in Real Time

Stan tried to explain to his friends what had happened. "They all got killed in a fire," he said. "I almost did, too."

"So you didn't end the feud?" Jared asked.

"I guess not," Stan said. "But I found out a lot of things."

He told Jared and Amy everything he'd been through. "And I saw you, too," he said. "I tried to get your attention, but you weren't aware of me."

"Who was the ghost?" Jared asked.

"You or us?"

Stan shrugged. "You looked like ghosts to me. But you never were. So maybe I was."

"So who really owned the orchard?" Amy asked. "The Fortins or the Wymans?"

"Randall Fortin finally told me that the Wymans owned it," Stan said. "But I think he was trying to trick me. He wanted me to distract the Wymans so he could burn the orchard down."

"Sounds crazy," Jared said. "He wound up killing them all."

"He said it was an accident, but I don't believe it," Stan said. "It's true that he tried to put the fire out. But it was too little, too late."

"I don't think he would have set it on fire if he owned it," Amy said.

Stan looked at the ground. He felt awful. Randall and the Wymans would have died anyway. He probably couldn't have changed that. But what about Josh? If Stan had warned him more strongly, he might have stayed away from the orchard that night.

"Did you see any ghosts while I was gone?" Stan asked.

"No," Jared replied. "It's been quiet."

"What time is it?"

"After ten," Amy said. "We should probably be getting home."

"This has been the worst night of my life," Stan said. "I could have saved a lot of lives. But I failed."

"They've been dead for a hundred years," Jared said. "You can't change history. All you did was witness it. You had no way to alter what happened."

"But I did," Stan said. "I spoke to all of them. I helped fight the fire."

"You were a ghost to them," Amy said. "No more real to them than they are to us."

That didn't make Stan feel any better.

He went home and showered, then climbed into bed. He lay awake thinking until nearly midnight.

Stan's Diary: Friday, September 25. (Back in real time!) 11:52 p.m.

This is hard to deal with. I know Josh wouldn't be alive anymore anyway. But only twelve years of life isn't enough. He deserved more.

What happened to the houses? Did the fire spread far enough to burn them up, too? That must have been the last night anyone lived on the hill. I hope the cow and the sheep escaped.

Stan turned out his light and tried to sleep. Every sound bothered him. Twice he was nearly asleep when he bolted up. Had someone been calling his name?

He finally dozed off, but he had another awful dream. This time he was standing on the bright side of the river. It was the present day. On the other side he could see Josh. Everything around him was in flames. Josh was standing at the river's edge, looking very fearful.

Stan yelled for Josh to jump into the raging river.

"I can't swim!" Josh called. "Come help me."

Stan pushed a canoe into the river and tried to paddle toward Josh. The current was very strong. The flames got closer to Josh and he jumped. He was carried quickly downstream.

Stan steered the canoe in the right direction and paddled harder. But Josh drifted farther away. Stan could hear him yelling, but he could not see him. And then the yelling stopped.

Stan woke up. He felt just as helpless as he had during the fire.

This was going to be a long night.

Chapter 14:
Josh's Hero

Stan's Diary: Saturday, September 26. 4:43 a.m.

Haven't slept much. It's not even dawn yet. As soon as there's some light, I'm going out there. I need to see if Josh has a gravestone. Maybe I missed it before. But I doubt it.

Lots of nightmares. I was chased. I was trapped. I was burned. And I was beaten up by the Wymans. I'm better off not even trying to sleep anymore.

When the first rays of sunlight turned the sky slightly pink, Stan put on a jacket and his hiking boots. He sneaked down the stairs and out the door.

Everything was quiet. The orchard area looked exactly the same. It was overgrown with brush. There were no apple trees. But Josh found the remains of the huge stump. It was right where the glowing apple tree had been.

He walked toward the Wyman area. He could see a few stones that had probably been part of the house's foundation. He'd seen the stones before, but they hadn't seemed important. The grave site looked the same.

But there was a difference. Stan glanced at the gravestones for Frederick, David, and Thomas. And then he looked again.

The dates were different! None of them had died on September 24. Frederick had lived for six more years. His sons had lived for nearly fifty.

"They survived the fire!" Stan shouted to the trees. "How can that be?"

He hurried across to the Fortins' area.

There were foundation stones there, too. But the house was long gone.

Randall's gravestone still said September 24. But now the year was ninety years ago. He'd lived for ten years after the fire.

Maybe Josh had survived, too!

But how would Stan ever know? There was no gravestone for Josh Fortin here. He couldn't still be alive. Could he?

What had happened? How could Stan find out?

He leaned against Randall's gravestone and stuck his hands in his pockets. He tried to think. And then he had an idea—Josh's grandfather!

The gravestone was still there, of course. Josh kneeled on the ground behind it. He lifted a stone. The small metal box was there.

Stan's hands were shaking as he lifted the lid. The notebook was there. It was stained and brittle, but it was intact.

I can't believe this! Stan thought. *I held this diary in my hand a hundred years ago.*

He opened the book and read the same entries he'd read before. And then he came to a new one.

September 24 (evening).

 The new boy is named Stan. I'm excited to have a boy my age in the neighborhood. He seems a bit odd, as if he's from far away. He says there is trouble coming tonight. He means the Wymans. We've asked him to speak to them for us. He said he has a bad feeling. I do, too. We must end this fight over the orchard.

There was only one more entry. Stan took a deep breath. He was almost afraid to read it. But he did.

September 26

 Two nights ago, the orchard burned to the ground. We barely escaped with our lives. My heart is aching. Stan led us out of the fire.

He said "Follow me" when the fire had us trapped. We ran behind him, and he led to us a small gap in the flames. We laid in the woods, barely able to think. We were panting and coughing. Our clothing was scorched. Finally we made our way to the Wymans' well and quenched our thirst. It was then that I realized Stan was not with us.

When the fire had burned out, we searched the area. There was no sign of him. Not even a trace of bone. The fire was very hot and it burned every tree to the ground. It took Stan with them.

We have no house left. Father and I have moved in with an uncle. The Wymans say they might rebuild their house. But they have no money. They are staying in town with relatives.

I feel terrible for Stan. We don't even know who he was. I went to the house he said he lived in, but no one knew of him. He must have been a homeless wanderer. I'm sure someone is missing him. But we may never know.

I'm leaving this diary here as a tribute to Stan. Perhaps someday *someone who knows him will come looking. If they find this box, they'll know that he was a hero.*

Some hero, Stan thought. *I ran for my life.* He shook his head. But somehow he had saved five lives. They'd all lived for years after that night.

Had the feud continued? Perhaps not, since it didn't seem as if anyone had lived on the hill after that night. Had the Wymans really replanted the orchard? Or had that only happened in the unreal past? The past that occurred after they all died in the fire. Things were different now. They hadn't died after all. So maybe the feud had ended.

It's all so confusing, Stan thought. He needed to find out what had become of Josh. Had he stayed in Marshfield? Was he buried somewhere else in town? And had he ever come back to this place on the hill? He'd left his diary behind. So maybe he'd never returned.

Stan didn't feel right about keeping the diary. He put it back in the box and placed it under the rock for now. But he needed to find a better place for it. With Josh.

"I'll find you," he said. "And when I do, we can all rest easy again."

Chapter 15:
My Friend for One Day

After breakfast, Stan was determined to find out what had happened to Josh. He grabbed his jacket and his bike. Soon, he was knocking on Amy's door. Amy's mom opened it.

"Hi, Mrs. Martinez. Is Amy home?" Stan asked.

"Sure, Stan. Just a minute," Mrs. Martinez said. Then she called out, "Amy, Stan is here."

Moments later, Stan and Amy were settled in the den. Stan wasn't sure how to ask his question, so he just blurted it out.

"How can we find out where somebody's buried?" he asked.

"It depends," Amy said. "If the town kept good records, it shouldn't be too hard. You can even find out online."

"Do you think we could do that now? I really need to know what happened to Josh," Stan asked hesitantly.

"Sure. Let's go to the computer room," Amy said. She led the way down the hall.

After the computer booted up, Amy pulled up the search engine and typed in "Marshfield Deaths." The first link that popped up led them to the town's records.

Stan guessed that Josh had probably died within the past thirty years.

"There," Amy said. She pointed to the screen. There were two Joshua Fortins listed. One of the dates seemed right for Josh's birth. He'd lived to age eighty-four.

"They're both buried in Hilltop," Stan

said. "But where?"

"Let's go look," Amy said. "We'll start by the orchard and fan out from there."

They went back to the Fortins' grave site and reread all of the stones. Josh was not buried here. But there were many other nearby gravestones.

Stan pointed to a group of stones about thirty yards away. "You look over there," he said. "I'll go up the hill."

All of the stones they looked at were from the past seventy years. This hadn't been a public cemetery a hundred years ago. Only the Fortins and Wymans had been buried here then.

Stan walked through the orchard area again. There was no sign that there had ever been a fire. But the ground was fertile. Lots of plants were growing. Most of them were weeds.

"Up here!" Amy shouted. She was waving her arms.

Stan hurried up the hill. Amy was standing in a small clearing. There were three gravestones in a neat row. It didn't look as if anyone had been up here for several years, but the stones were straight and clean. The cleared spot was only about as big as Stan's bedroom. The earth was covered with soft green moss. Tall pines kept the clearing partly hidden.

Amy pointed to the three stones.

JOSHUA FORTIN SR.
MARTHA BROWN FORTIN
JOSHUA FORTIN JR.

"Wow," Stan said. Martha had been Josh's wife. And Josh Jr. was obviously their son. He'd died about ten years ago.

"So Josh did make it back up here," Amy said.

Stan nodded. He kneeled on the moss in front of Josh's grave. "Hope you had a good life," he said. "I'm sure you did."

He found a flat rock and dug a hole behind Josh's gravestone. Then he ran back and got the metal box.

"What's that?" Amy asked.

Stan debated telling Amy. He knew he could trust her. "Don't ever tell anyone about this," he said. He let her read the diary entries.

Amy smiled. "So, you're a hero," she said.

Stan frowned. "Josh thinks I was. I'm not so sure."

"I think you did all right," Amy said.

"All in a night's work," Stan replied sheepishly.

They buried the box.

"I'll come back up here often," Stan said. He pointed to Josh's grave. "He was my friend for one day."

"I'm sure he never forgot you," Amy said.

They stood by the graves for a few minutes longer, looking down the hill toward the orchard.

"You know what?" Stan said. "I'll bet apple trees would still grow there. The ground is good. There's enough sunlight."

"You're probably right."

"It would be nice for Josh's family to be near a thriving orchard again," Stan said. "Let's plant some trees in the springtime. It might be a few years before they produce any apples, but that's okay."

"You really like apples all of a sudden, huh?" Amy said.

"I'll tell you one thing," Stan said. "The apples from that orchard were the best I've ever eaten. I only had two, but they were sweet and tangy and full of juice."

"Sounds delicious," Amy said. "Makes me want an apple right now."

"Me too," Stan said. "I guess we could go buy some. Won't be quite the same, but they'll have to do for now."

"Until the new trees are ready?"

"Yeah," Stan said. "But I can wait." He laughed. "I've been waiting a hundred years for another taste of those apples. I guess a few more years won't hurt."

Time Travel
from Stan Summer

Step 1: Approach a glowing, ghostly object with caution. It could be a time portal.

Step 2: Brace yourself if the air is suddenly very cold.

Step 3: There will be a bright flash of light, and then everything will go dark.

Step 4: You will feel yourself falling. You will hear a squishing sound just before you land on the ground.

Step 5: When you land, make sure to look around before you move around. The new time period may have a different landscape than you are used to. For example, an apple orchard may have popped up where there used to be a field!

Step 6: Carefully approach people you meet. They may talk differently, wear different clothing, or fear strangers.

Step 7: Watch for the portal that will return you to your time period. It may arrive when you least expect it.

Ghost Facts
from Stan Summer

#1: Not all ghosts are angry.

#2: Angry ghosts may just be holding a hundred-year-old grudge. Be respectful to show you aren't involved in the feud.

#3: Most ghosts are see-through. However, they have been known to throw solid objects. That hurts!

#4: Sometimes a ghost will appear solid. Usually you can tell they are a ghost when they disappear in a snap.

#5: Helping a ghost find peace is the best way to put them to rest. Sometimes that means doing things you aren't used to—like time travel.

About the ...

Author

Baron Specter is the pen name of Rich Wallace, who has written many novels for kids and teenagers. His latest books include the Kickers soccer series and the novel *Sports Camp*.

Illustrator

Setch Kneupper has years of experience thinking he saw a ghost, although Graveyard Diaries is the first series of books he's illustrated about the ordeal.